This
Treasure Cove Story
belongs to

_____

LADY AND THE TRAMP

A CENTUM BOOK 978-1-912396-25-2
Published in Great Britain by Centum Books Ltd.
This edition published 2018.

3 5 7 9 10 8 6 4

Centum Books Ltd, 20 Devon Square, Newton Abbot,
Devon, TQ12 2HR, UK.

www.centumbooksltd.co.uk | books@centumbooksltd.co.uk
CENTUM BOOKS Limited Reg.No. 07641486.

A CIP catalogue record for this book is available
from the British Library.

Printed in China.

centum

A Treasure Cove Story

Walt Disney's

Lady and the
TRAMP

Adapted by Teddy Slater
Illustrated by Bill Langley and Ron Dias

Lady was a lucky little cocker spaniel. She had everything a dog could want. Her beloved owners, Jim Dear and Darling, had pampered her since puppyhood. They gave her the tastiest tidbits to eat and the softest bed to sleep in and they showered her with affection.

Lady returned this kindness by waking her master each morning with a gentle lick on the cheek. And while he was at work, Lady stayed close to her mistress, protecting her from possible harm.

But one day, everything changed. As Lady told her
friends, Trusty and Jock, Darling now seemed more
interested in the tiny sweater she was knitting than in her
faithful friend.

Lady's pals quickly put two and two together and figured
out that Darling was going to have a baby.

'Babies are mighty sweet,' Trusty the bloodhound said.
'And very, very soft,' Jock the Scottie added. 'Why,
a wee babe is nothin' but a bundle of...'

'...trouble!' an unfamiliar voice chimed in.

The voice belonged to a scruffy stranger named Tramp. Though Tramp had no family of his own, he seemed to know quite a lot about babies – and none of it was good.

'Take it from me, Pigeon,' Tramp told Lady. 'A human heart has only so much room for love and affection. When a baby moves in, the dog moves out!'

Although Tramp's words worried Lady, she couldn't believe that her family would ever be unkind. And once the baby was born, Lady saw just how wrong Tramp had been. For not only did Lady still have her family's love, she now had one more person to cherish and protect.

Everything was fine until Jim Dear and Darling decided to take a short holiday.

'Don't worry, old girl,' Jim Dear told Lady before they left. 'Aunt Sarah will be staying here to care for you and the baby.'

But Aunt Sarah soon made it clear that she did not
like dogs at all. To make matters worse, she had brought
her two nasty cats along. Lady watched helplessly as they
wrecked the living room and terrorized the goldfish
and the bird.

When the cats headed upstairs, however, Lady sprang into action. She raced ahead to stop them from entering the nursery. The nasty creatures tried to run by her, but Lady stopped them in their tracks with a threatening growl.

Aunt Sarah heard the commotion and poked her head out of the nursery. She took one look at Lady growling and the two cats snivelling and she ran to protect her pets.

'Oh, my precious pusses,' she crooned. And scooping the cats up in her arms, she carried them gently downstairs.

Then Aunt Sarah dragged Lady off to the pet store.

'I want a muzzle for this vicious beast,' she told the salesman.

'I have just the thing,' the man replied, placing one of the awful contraptions over the struggling dog's face.

In desperation, poor Lady ran out of the store.

Outside, a pack of stray dogs began to chase her. Horns
blared and tyres screeched as Lady raced blindly through
the streets, across the railway tracks and into a strange and
scary part of town.

Her heart pounding, Lady ran on with the strays yapping at her heels. Just when she felt she couldn't take another step, a brown ball of fur rushed to her side.

Biting and barking, Tramp fought off Lady's attackers until every last one had turned tail and slunk away.

Tramp helped Lady remove the hateful muzzle and
then she told him her tale of woe.

'Poor Pidge,' he said when she had finished her story.
'You sure have had a terrible day. What you need
is a night out on the town to cheer you up!'

Tramp led Lady to a quaint little Italian restaurant.
There they shared a delicious plate of spaghetti and
meatballs while musicians serenaded them with
a romantic tune.

After dinner, Lady and Tramp took a moonlight stroll. When they came to a patch of wet cement, Tramp scratched a big heart in the middle and placed one of his paws inside it. Lady did the same.

A silvery moon was high in the sky when the two tired dogs finally snuggled up under a tree and fell fast asleep.

When they awoke the next morning, Lady was horrified to realize she had spent the whole night away from home.

'Aw, Pidge,' Tramp said, 'there's a big wide world out there just waiting for us. Why go back at all?'

'Because my family needs me,' Lady replied. 'And I need them. Besides, who will protect the baby if I'm not there?'

Tramp had no answer for that. He simply bowed his head in defeat. And even though Lady was sad to leave Tramp, she could hardly wait to return to her family.

But when Lady got home, an angry Aunt Sarah was waiting for her. 'I have a special place for you now,' Aunt Sarah snapped as she led Lady to a dog kennel in the back garden. 'This should keep you out of trouble!' she said, chaining Lady to a stake in the ground.

That night Lady was moping around the back
garden when a big grey rat scurried out of the woodpile,
scampered up the porch railing and darted into an
upstairs window.

'That's the baby's room!' Lady cried. She dashed
forward but was jerked to a painful halt by her chain.
Lady barked frantically to attract Aunt Sarah's attention.

Aunt Sarah finally appeared at the back door, but only to yell at Lady. 'Stop that racket!' she said before slamming the door again.

Just then, Tramp raced into the garden. He had heard Lady barking and had come to help her once more.

'There's a rat in the baby's room!' Lady said. And with no thought for his own safety, Tramp ran inside to get the rat.

Tramp reached the nursery in the nick of time. The baby lay sleeping in the crib, and the rat was ready to pounce.

Tramp struck first. Fur flew and furniture fell as dog and rat tore around the room. The rat was fast and fierce, but he was no match for Tramp.

By the time Aunt Sarah burst in, there was no sign of the rat – just Tramp and the topsy-turvy room. Aunt Sarah thought that Tramp had been after the baby and she quickly called the dogcatcher.

'Don't come back, you vicious brute,' Aunt Sarah warned as Tramp was carried off to the pound.

As soon as Lady explained what had happened, Trusty and Jock took off after Tramp. They chased the dogcatcher through the dark and stormy night.

When a taxi appeared out of the fog, the dogcatcher's horses reared up and his wagon toppled over. Jim Dear and Darling were in the taxi. They had come home and discovered the rat. It was clear then that Tramp had been protecting the baby and they went after him. He was a true hero!

Jim Dear and Darling decided to take Tramp into
their home.

'This is where you belong,' Jim Dear told Tramp.
'You're part of our family now.'

And soon Lady and Tramp had a family of their own
– three pretty pups, who looked just like their mother and
one mischievous Scamp, who clearly took after his father.

Treasure Cove Stories

Please contact Centum Books
to receive the full list of titles in
the *Treasure Cove Stories* series.
books@centumbooksltd.co.uk

Classic favourites

1 Three Little Pigs
2 Snow White and
the Seven Dwarfs
3 The Fox and the Hound
- Hide-and-Seek
4 Dumbo
5 Cinderella
6 Cinderella's Friends
7 Alice in Wonderland
8 Mad Hatter's Tea Party
from Alice in Wonderland
9 Mickey Mouse and
his Spaceship
10 Peter Pan
11 Pinocchio
12 Mickey and the Beanstalk
13 Sleeping Beauty
and the Good Fairies
14 The Lucky Puppy
15 Chicken Little
16 The Incredibles
17 Coco
18 Winnie the Pooh and Tigger
19 The Sword in the Stone
20 Mary Poppins
21 The Jungle Book
22 The Aristocats
23 Lady and the Tramp
24 Bambi
25 Bambi - Friends of the Forest

Recently published

50 Frozen
51 Cinderella is my Babysitter
52 Beauty and the Beast
- I am the Beast
53 Blaze and the Monster Machines
- Mighty Monster Machines
54 Blaze and the Monster Machines
- Dino Parade!
55 Teenage Mutant Ninja Turtles
- Follow the Ninja!

56 I am a Princess
57 The Big Book of Paw Patrol
58 Paw Patrol
- Adventures with Grandpa!
59 Paw Patrol - Pirate Pups!
60 Trolls
61 Trolls Holiday
62 The Secret Life of Pets
63 Zootropolis
64 Ariel is my Babysitter
65 Tiana is my Babysitter
66 Belle is my Babysitter
67 Paw Patrol
- Itty-Bitty Kitty Rescue
68 Moana
69 Nella the Princess Knight
- My Heart is Bright!
70 Guardians of the Galaxy
71 Captain America
- High-Stakes Heist!
72 Ant-Man
73 The Mighty Avengers
74 The Mighty Avengers
- Lights Out!
75 The Incredible Hulk
76 Shimmer & Shine
- Wish Upon a Sleepover
77 Shimmer & Shine - Backyard Ballet
78 Paw Patrol - All-Star Pups!
79 Teenage Mutant Ninja Turtles
- Really Spaced Out!
80 I am Ariel
81 Madagascar
82 Jasmine is my Babysitter
83 How to Train your Dragon
84 Shrek
85 Puss in Boots
86 Kung Fu Panda
87 Beauty and the Beast - I am Belle
88 The Lion Guard
- The Imaginary Okapi
89 Thor - Thunder Strike!
90 Guardians of the Galaxy
- Rocket to the Rescue!
91 Nella the Princess Knight
- Nella and the Dragon
92 Shimmer & Shine
- Treasure Twins!

93 Olaf's Frozen Adventure
94 Black Panther
95 Trolls
- Branch's Bunker Birthday
96 Trolls - Poppy's Party
97 The Ugly Duckling
98 Cars - Look Out for Mater!
99 101 Dalmatians
100 The Sorcerer's Apprentice
101 Tangled
102 Avengers
- The Threat of Thanos
103 Puppy Dog Pals
- Don't Rain on my Pug-Rade
104 Jurassic Park
105 The Mighty Thor
106 Doctor Strange

Latest publications

107 Captain Marvel
108 The Invincible Iron Man
109 Black Panther
- Warriors of Wakanda
110 The Big Freeze
111 Ratatouille
112 Aladdin
113 Aladdin - I am the Genie
114 Seven Dwarfs Find a House
115 Toy Story
116 Toy Story 4
117 Paw Patrol - Jurassic Bark!
118 Paw Patrol
- Mighty Pup Power!
119 Shimmer & Shine
- Pet Talent Show!
120 SpongeBob SquarePants
- Krabby Patty Caper
121 The Lion King - I am Simba
122 Winnie the Pooh
- The Honey Tree
123 Frozen II
124 Baby Shark and the
Colours of the Ocean
125 Baby Shark and
the Police Sharks!
126 Trolls World Tour

Book list may be subject to change.